Picking Up From The Broken Pieces

INSPIRATIONAL ROMANCE NOVEL

♥

ANGELA C. GRIFFITHS

1st Printing

PICKING UP FROM THE BROKEN PIECES
INSPIRATIONAL ROMANCE NOVEL

ISBN: 979-8-218-46446-2

Published by Angela C. Griffiths

Dedications

I dedicate this book to all the single individuals who will read this book, I wrote this book with you in mind to give you hope while you wait for that special person, so you can dream while you wait on that soulmate, that Ruth and Boaz.

Acknowledgement

I give thanks to the Lord who gave me the vision to write these books. And a special thanks to Mr. Samuel. O, who always encourages me from the beginning.

Table Of Contents

1 THE MISSION TRIP 1

2 HER ASSIGNMENT 7

3 BIRTH DURING CATASTROPHE 10

4 THE ABDUCTION 16

5 OVERWHELMING FEAR 20

6 THE KNOCK AND ESCAPE 27

7 THE PLEA 34

8 A QUIET PLACE TO TALK 44

9 THE UNPLANNED SEXUAL ENCOUNTER 50

10 GOING HOME 56

11 THE LOOK 63

12 THE ARRIVAL HOME 70

13 THE LAKE VISIT 76

"Love is that condition in which the happiness of another person is essential to your own."

- Robert A. Heinlein

1 THE MISSION TRIP

Strolling on the beautiful white sand beach, Gabrielle thought about all she had been through as she gently placed her feet and toes in the sand of the warm, salted water. It was a perfect temperature of 80 degrees. The sun was setting beyond the borders of the water as far as her eyes could see, the orange-colored sunrays setting in the distance as it went down. She reminisced on picking up from the broken pieces, playing like a little girl in the aqua blue waters, splashing and kicking her feet. It had been years since her last visit to the ocean; she was now like a child visiting for the very first time. As the tall, dark, and handsome man observed her beauty.

"Here she goes again, always running to help someone, every chance she gets. That's my Gabrielle," her mother said. "She was born for that purpose, I guess," her mother and aunt whispered to each other as she packed her bags and got ready to head out to the airport. "She is always giving, to the loss and unfortunate, the helpless, the homeless," her auntie replied. "That's a good thing," her sister replied as well. As the conversation continued, her mom stated, "It always seems as though the one that does the greater good always seems to be the one that suffers the most." They all agreed as they talked about a few things that happened in her past, but she is a strong woman. She just brushed herself off and kept on going. "Yes! She is," they all agreed.

Gabrielle volunteered twice per month at her local soup kitchen to help the homeless, the hopeless, in her local community. On Sundays after church service, she sometimes served meals and gave out clothing to the less fortunate. Now, nature calls again, and she joins her church group and other local churches in the community that put together money and supplies for natural disasters, such as the one she is heading out to give a helping hand. "I am all packed and ready to go," she yelled. She was excited and so happy to go. This was her second trip out of the country helping disaster victims, but she gets joy and pleasure naturally helping others. "Before you go," her mother exclaimed, "let's pray and send up a prayer first before you go for protection." As they walked into her room, they gathered around her, holding hands to pray. "Dear Lord, as my daughter is about to take her journey on her way to help the more needy of your children that are desperately in need, please cover and protect mine and bring her back safely home and the others that are reaching out to help and to bring her home safely once again. Thank you, God, for hearing and answering my prayer ahead of time concerning my daughter." She quickly hugged her mom, sister, and auntie and kissed them farewell.

As the van with a group of volunteers pulled up to her gate, they helped her downstairs with her luggage to the van. She gave her emergency contact information to her mom as she quickly hopped into the van. Her mom had a sad and concerned look on her face, but Gabrielle assured her all would be well, and it is for a good cause. She smiled as she waved goodbye. Gabrielle comforted her mom once again with a smile, stating all is well. What? Her mom worried about her daughter because she is the last of two girls and the only one with a heart of gold. She then whispered a prayer once again in her heart.

It was a long ride to the airport, a very tiring trip. But Gabrielle was excited, chatting as they rode to the airport, getting acquainted with her other fellow volunteers. She did not care about where they were going if they were all safe and anticipated to get started. She visualized what she would be doing as work, the people she would be helping, and the ones she would meet during her travels. Her passion and desires were working with children. She loved children and had a heart of compassion to help them. By the time she looked ahead, they were already at the airport. The attendant assisted her with their luggage, and the group hurried to check in and board the plane, and off they went.

On her way to the Caribbean Island, it took several hours before they arrived at their destination. The disaster struck; this was not just a casual vacation but a critical emergency that was deemed for those who have a heart for people and wanted to give back purely from the heart, not for accolades and to be commended. As she sat on the flight, she thought of her mother and the look on her face, purely of concern. But she prayed also that the good Lord would give her peace. It was a few hours, and they finally landed on the severely devastated and ravished island from the earthquake. Awaiting as they landed was another group of volunteers from other countries, states, and provinces coming from almost everywhere to help. They were separated into groups based on occupation and needs.

They all gathered in large hallways filled with supplies and their clothing awaiting the arrival of the ground transportation to pick them up and take them to the destination of the most priority. But while they were waiting, they were ushered to another area while they waited, a cafeteria to eat and rest while they waited to get picked up. They saw pictures of some of the most devastated areas. Shortly after, they were picked up and transported to their hotel where they would rest for the night. She called her mother and informed her they arrived safely and had to begin their assignment early in the morning because it was already too late in the evening when they arrived to do anything; her mom was very happy to hear from her, chat for a while, then said good night.

Gabrielle was very excited, anticipating the assignment she was about to undertake, hoping she would be taking care of some children or babies she loved dearly. She talked and got acquainted with a few of her fellow volunteers while they ate and waited for their transportation to arrive. She was able to contact her mom to let her know they arrived safe, but the connection was not very good due to the severely damaged towers in the area. The bus finally arrived shortly afterward and took them to their hotels. It was a short distance from the airport, but the island was ravaged; the devastation was enormous. People were walking the streets with all they had left. The hotel was very nice and clean. It was not the upscale standard she was used to in the states, but she was thankful, seeing the many that lost everything and have no place to live. She was saddened to see such loss and devastation. She finally settled in the hotel and had something to eat, but her mind was not at ease at what she observed on her way to the hotel. She was too tired from the long trip, so she settled in and went to bed early so she would be well-rested for her assignment in the morning.

"Love is shown more in deeds than in words."

- Saint Ignatius

2 HER ASSIGNMENT

Gabriel arose early the next morning, anticipating her day. She was very anxious to start on her assignment. They all gathered and met in the breakfast pavilion where they had their assignments handed to them for the day. They had their breakfast, and shortly thereafter, a bus arrived and picked them up from the front of the hotel and took them to their assigned destination.

It was a makeshift clinic and food bank that supplied food, clothing, and medical supplies to care for the needy and injured. As she started the day, she was happy but sad because of the many people who had lost their lives and many who were injured and desperately in need of help. The team gathered into small groups of five and dispersed themselves in specific areas of interest, expertise, and most urgent need.

Gabrielle dove in and fitted right in. She got the assignment she wanted and was very happy where she was placed. The clinic door was open, and the injured started to come in from near and far, all areas of town and cities. Those that were severely injured for care in the clinic were sent out to the local hospital nearby. The children and babies poured in groves, long lines outside and around the building. She took care of the babies, some with broken bones, some with vomiting and diarrhea, and some with fever from drinking the polluted dirty water. She fell in love with a few of the babies and their families. They were thankful and humble. When a case came in that was very severe, it was painful, and the suffering was intense. She would go into the restroom and cry, then return and encourage an attendant to help the injured.

The first day was rough. She saw many new cases and things that day and gained experience she was never exposed to before. That evening, when she went to the hotel and rested, she thought about some of the cases that she encountered that day. A few days went by as the volunteers got acquainted and worked together well for the cause.

"Where there is great love there are always great miracles."

-Willa Cather

3 BIRTH DURING CATASTROPHE

It was about two weeks into Gabrielle's assignment. She was attending to the babies, which she loved! She was enjoying her work, working hand in hand with the other volunteers and enjoying the children and her co-volunteers. One afternoon, while she was attending to a baby, a man came in with his pregnant wife who was in labor. She quickly finished what she was doing for the child and helped attend to the woman and her husband. The rest of the volunteers did their assignment and acknowledged the child and mother were in distress and an immediate decision must be made to spare the lives of both mother and baby. Gabrielle notified the physician immediately and assisted him with the care of this woman and her child. The father and husband were called in so the doctor could explain the urgency, evaluate the situation, and explain that immediate actions must be taken for them to save the mother and the child's life.

But while they were attending to the mother, the situation took a turn for the worse. The mother was at 9 centimeters dilation and delivered the baby imminently. The baby was in a breach position, feet first, and another doctor was notified to come in and help. They tried to start the delivery to do a cesarean section, but the baby was in severe distress and the heartbeat was dropping fast. They had to make a quick decision and escort the father outside to the waiting room. They attended to the mother who was now in severe distress. They tried their best to attend and care for the mother and the baby by doing a quick cesarean section, but the mother was in major distress. She had a heart attack delivering the baby.

The child was in distress as well; to decrease oxygen, the umbilical cord was choking the life out of the child. They finally revived him with oxygen, but the mother did not make it. She died on the table due to severe loss of blood. They were all devastated because of this. This was the first time they had experienced anything like this. They wrapped the baby up in a blanket and Gabrielle and another attending physician went out with the baby and handed the child to the father. He was very happy. He took the child quickly from them and cuddled, hugged, and kissed him on his forehead. "It's a boy," he said, finally realizing he had a son, with a smile on his face.

"How is my wife doing?" he asked. Then there was a silence, a brief silence in the room. A look of apprehension and anxiety came over the father's face. The silence: he knew something was wrong, but he didn't know what. The attending physician broke the silence and braced himself to tell the father the bad news. He spoke with a soft voice. "We tried our very best, we tried hard to save her, but she was in severe distress when she came in." The doctor didn't complete the sentence and started to scream and yell for his wife and held his head while the nurse quickly took and held the child while he wept. The doctor continued to talk softly and tried to apologize and comfort him. He screamed even more for his wife in disbelief. He cried and ran to the room to see her and to see if all this was truly happening. He cried louder and grabbed her and held her tightly.

He took the baby and held him in his arms close to the mother while he cried aloud. He then passed the child to Gabrielle once again while he cried and held his wife tightly and talked. The doctor stood by, speechless, with tears in their eyes, as did Gabrielle as she held the baby in her arms to comfort him.

The father said as he held his wife in his arms, "It is not fair. You can't leave us like this, you can't leave us alone. Come back. Come back to us. We have tried for so long to have this little bundle of joy and now you are leaving us! How am I? How are we? Going to live without you?" As he sobbed, Gabrielle gave him a tissue to wipe away his tears and gently hugged him and gave her condolences once again.

The doctors tried to console him, but he was not consolable. He finally sat down, and Gabrielle talked with him for a while to console him and give him the child and encouraged him to hold the baby and love him. He looked at her and smiled and took the baby from her arms, kissed, and talked with him. He finally calmed down a bit and said, "It will be okay! Mother has left us, so we are now on our own," as he wiped away the tears from his eyes. He seemed to be okay and accepted that she was gone.

The group stepped out of the room to give the young father privacy, time, and space to say goodbye to his wife because it was now late in the evening for the clinic to close and also for them to talk and grieve the loss and go to the hotel. They stepped away. He lost control again, crying out loud, talking and praying. The group remained close by but enough distance for time and privacy. He held his son tightly. Some of his and her family arrived. They stayed together, bonded, and comforted each other, while the group hugged and cried together about what had happened to the young woman. They were distraught. It was time to go as they said goodbye to the family, and the child was released into his care.

As the days passed by, things got easier for the group and better with the cleaning up of the cities and counties. But the death of the young woman bothered them all. That night when they arrived at their hotel to rest, they were all restless and found it hard to sleep. As the days passed by, things became easier and better with the cleanup and rebuilding of the towns and country. A few weeks later, the young man brought the child in for follow-up care. It was Gabrielle who took care of him. It was awkward to talk about his loss, but she did and broke the silence, but he was reluctant to talk about it, so she stayed quiet and changed the subject. But she referred him to some community services for those who are grieving the loss of loved ones from the devastation of the hurricane.

He spoke and said thank you for the information and took the child and said goodbye. She was happy to see the baby was growing and doing well. She was happy for that reason but was also sad for the young man and his loss. But she was also a bit concerned about him, but there was not anything else she could do to help him. Things were improving and going well. She was happy to be there helping the less fortunate. She missed her family and friends back home, but the days were winding down, and the trip was coming to an end, and a new group of volunteers was on their way to take their place. Some evenings after work, Gabrielle would take long walks, looking around the community and the devastation of the country. Each time she went to walk, her spirit was grieved and hurting because of the people. Her heart went out to them. Reports were lost in the devastation of her surroundings. That evening she got sidetracked and lost track of time. It was getting late and soon to be dark, so she hurried towards her hotel. Suddenly, she saw a shadow lurking closely behind her. As she turned to see who it was, she felt a tugging.

"For God has not given us a spirit of fear,
but of power, love and a sound mind."

- 2 Timothy 1:7 KJV

4 THE ABDUCTION

Fear started to set in. She was not worried about her life, but about her family's pain, hurt, and anguish if something was to happen to her so far away, outside the country. Tears started to flow down her face as she breathed fast and shallowly. The abductor did not speak, not a word. She figured in her mind that's because he or she wanted to disguise their voice so they wouldn't be familiar in any way. Gabrielle, even though she was crying, started to wonder to herself, "Why would anyone want to kidnap me? My family is not well off for any major ransom." Then just as her thoughts ended, she noticed the truck started to slow down. Now she was even more afraid, and fear gripped her heart. A thousand things ran across her mind as she wondered what next? The truck finally came to a complete stop. The abductor pushed his door open and got out and walked towards the back where she sat. She could hear the footsteps coming closer towards the back door.

Finally, the door was open, and the abductor pulled her towards the edge of the seat. Gabrielle tossed and turned as she tried to scream and pull away. She was dragged closer to the edge of her seat as she tried to pull away in the opposite direction. As this was happening, she cried out to God in her heart. "God, protect me. Let no harm come to your daughter. Help me! Keep a watch over me. Let me not be afraid, Lord! Why does this evil come upon me? As I came securely and purely to do a good work and deed. Please bring peace and comfort to my heart and mind in all this turmoil. Let me live to see daybreak and freedom again. Thank you for listening to my prayers. Amen!" As the abductor pulled her off the seat into his arms, she did not fight and stayed calm and quiet because she knew who had her back. There was peace after she prayed, a peace that came over her she could not explain or understand.

She walked a few steps with the abductor holding her in his arms. Shortly after, he stopped and put her down to stand up. It seemed to be an entrance of some sort, the entrance of a door possibly, because she could hear the rattling of keys, then the screeching as the door was pushed open. So, Gabrielle had no idea where she was. She didn't know if she was in the same city or another town, but based on the drive, it didn't seem to be very far away from where she was abducted.

The abductor did not talk at all. She surmised he was afraid she may recognize his voice. Eventually, she was led to the entrance of a room that had a spice-like fragrance that smelled like apple, cinnamon, and peaches. The blindfold was removed quickly, and she was thrust forward quickly into the room. It had a bed, a chair, table, and a small lamp. The room was well-lit with light, but whoever it was disappeared quickly out of sight, not to be seen or heard. Then she said to herself, "Maybe whoever it is doesn't want to hurt me?! But why this?" She finally sat on the chair, overlooking the decor of the small room. It was very quiet, not even a footstep present. She turned the old radio on, but it was just static and a few stations that played only Latin music. She did not understand very well. Two hours had passed, then she heard footsteps coming closer towards the door as though they were walking down a stairwell. She was very afraid because she did not know what was next. Finally, a door was opened, and someone walked in and placed something on the floor, knocked on the door, as she was about to open it, they disappeared.

As she looked towards the floor, there was a small tray of water and food. Beyond that was another door that was locked. She prayed over the food before she took any because she was very hungry at this time. She thought about her fellow volunteers if they were looking for her because it was about time for dinner. Then they all meet up and eat together in the large pavilion of the hotel they stayed at this time. Gabrielle was also very concerned about her family, thinking about their sorrows, and worrying about her disappearance.

"When I am afraid, I will put my
trust and faith in you."

- Psalms 56:3 AMP

5 OVERWHELMING FEAR

Suddenly, she heard footsteps once again. It sounded like whoever was coming downstairs, and the door opened! Gabrielle was now afraid because she did not know what to expect this time. As the sound of keys entered the door entrance of the room she was staying in, she moved away from the entrance of the door to the furthest corner of the room. She heard voices speaking in English and Spanish. A door was now open, and a bright light was shining in her face, so she was unable to recognize anyone that entered the room. The English voices spoke and told her to turn around so they could once again blindfold her. She did as she was told, fearfully and sighing, shaking in fear. They held her hand and led her out of the room a few feet away, and she counted the steps just to keep her mind focused as she passed through what seemed to be a small passageway. She heard a crying child. She continued to walk as they slowed down and then stopped. Once again, sounds of keys were heard, entering and opening what seemed to be a door. She was pushed in quickly as other voices were close by in the vicinity. Gabrielle was now very afraid. She was told to be quiet and not to remove the blindfold until she was told to do so. She was given a small morsel of food and a bed. She sat on it while waiting in the room.

As she sat, her mind wandered, and she relapsed into periods of her past, being locked in a room and blindfolded. At this present situation, this was done to her by her verbally and physically abusive widowed husband. She remembered the voice saying, "You are my wife, and I will never let you go. If I can't have you, no one will." After he locked her in the basement for months, she attempted to escape several times, and finally, after the third attempt, she was successful. Her family at the time thought she was dead after many attempts to find her. They placed flyers, media coverage, and asked friends to help find her. No one suspected that it was her estranged husband abusing her because she was afraid and told no one. After her escape, she broke the horrible news to her family, and no law enforcement was involved, but her husband was nowhere to be found. He left the state and eventually the country. She was still apprehensive, fearful, and trusted no one. After a few months, she divorced him and moved on with what was left of her life.

One day, she was on her way home after work. She was in a hurry to get home. She noticed a car in the distance, but she could not see the person's face. As she continued driving, they turned off the road and went in another direction. The following weekend, tired from work, she pulled into her driveway and opened the trunk of her car to pick up her groceries. As she climbed the steps, holding keys in one hand and groceries in the next, attempting to open the front door, she saw a shadow of a person from the side and grabbed her. She screamed and dropped her groceries, trying to hurry and open the door. The voice uttered, "You thought you were going to get away from me! You thought you would be free from me?" She suddenly recognized the voice. In terror, she screamed, pawing at the door, holding onto the screen door as he pulled her towards him. "Help! Help!" she cried and screamed, hoping someone would hear her and come to her rescue.

She fought as hard as she could to get away from him, but he pulled on her legs, trying to pull her down the steps. She thought, "If he gets me to himself this time, I don't believe I'll make it out alive this time." As she screamed even louder, the police sirens sounded, but he would not let her go. The police tried to stop him, but he pulled out a knife and tried to stab her. They pulled their weapons, warned him to drop his knife, he did not, and they discharged their weapon at him. He died on the spot, grasping and holding onto her legs. She was in major pain in her heart, hurting because she loved her husband, but he was abusive, and she had to let him go.

So, Gabrielle cried loudly, hurting and in pain, because she was reminiscing about that ordeal then and at the present time. She finally pulled the blindfold off her eyes and cried. That night, she was not able to sleep well but kept rehashing the scenes over and over in her mind of the last moment of her ex-husband's death and his attempt to kidnap her.

She was awakened once again by the cries of a child coming from across the way. The room was warm and cozy. She was wondering in her heart, speaking to the Lord, "Help me to find a way out of here." As she prayed, the cries of the child kept coming in her ears. Gabrielle started to say to herself, "Something must be wrong with that child crying like that. I hope everything is alright." She said to herself, compassion creeping into her heart due to the cries of the child. "Poor soul. That poor child." As she wondered if it was hungry or hurting, she whispered a prayer as she prayed for herself. Shortly after, she heard footsteps once again and the cry of the child coming closer to her door, as if they were passing by the small room. But instead, wherever they were, they stopped, and she heard the keys once again opening the locks to her door. As they entered this time, they had masked faces. They requested her to step back, step away from the door. She was very afraid, but a small child they had in a basket, covered with a blanket, still crying.

She figured it was the child that she heard. This was the child that had been crying and awakened her. They pushed the basket towards her with the child in it and a small bag that had food, formula, diapers, and some clothing. They dropped it on the floor and backed away quickly out of the room. Gabrielle was surprised. She got closer to the basket and uncovered the crying child. She recognized the baby! It was the handsome baby boy from the clinic that they delivered a few weeks ago when the mom died delivering him. But she could not quite remember which family he belonged to. She was now more focused on helping the poor baby to calm down and stop crying. She stretched her hands to pick him up. Few realized the reason for the continual crying. The baby was running a fever, and she had nothing but a bottle of water. She tried banging on the door to get the masked men's attention. That's a child who needed medical help beyond what she was able to do, but no one answered or came back. Gabriel did all she could to comfort the baby, but he continued to cry. She poured the bottle of water she had on the blanket and took his clothes off, trying to keep him cool from his head to his feet to break the fever. While she prayed and tried to sing and hush him in comfort, she cried, "Oh Lord, help this innocent child. Don't let him die in my arms. You are the healer. Seeing the situation of the child, Father, I thank you for listening to me. Don't let him die. Please, thanks for hearing my prayers." As she continued to hush, sing, and pray, she stopped for a while and fed him, and that did help a little because he seemed to be hungry as well. As she fed him, Gabrielle remembered the family whose child this baby belonged to. "Oh Lord! For sure," she said to herself. "It was the family that lost the mother during the birth of this child." Gabrielle was now getting fearful because she knew who it was that left the child. But a peace suddenly came over her that all is well, so she continued to pray over the baby boy and continued the sponge bath to help break his fever. Eventually, he fell asleep, and she placed him on the bed in his basket. She now started to wonder, was this the reason for her being kidnapped?

She did not let the fear overwhelm her. She thought to herself, "But at least I have some company temporarily." "God?" she said. "I want to get out of here. I miss my family and friends. I want to go home. I know they are worried about me." She started to cry, then pray. "Lord, keep my family in peace. Don't let my mom die worrying about me. Please make a way for me to escape this horrible trap."

This went on for days. The fever finally broke in the child. It was about two more weeks that she was locked in. At this time, the volunteers Gabriel was working with had been looking for her. They were finally able to reach her family. They flew down to the island and were searching for her, as well as the police of that town. They all got involved because they knew the community and that they had been coming for many years to help the country. Now it was easier to get around because all the debris was now cleared in that area, and all things were almost back to normal on the roads, except lights and water. What are some of the major breakdowns in some buildings? Every evening, they would go out with the family and friends and volunteers for about two to four hours after work, going door to door asking if anyone saw her. Anne was showing her pictures, asking the neighbors if they had seen or recognized Gabriel.

"Trust in the Lord with all your heart and
lean not unto your own understanding.
In all thy ways acknowledge him,
and he shall direct thy paths."

- Proverb 3:5

6 THE KNOCK AND ESCAPE

One evening, after the masked men stopped by with food, clothing, and diapers for the child and for Gabrielle, there was a knock on the door leading to the hallway where she was located. It was the police, and sirens going off startled the men, causing them to take the child and run away, fearing they would be caught, leaving the door ajar. It was not completely locked, and Gabriel noticed it. She slowly tiptoed towards the door and peeked out through the small opening, but no one was there in the hallway or anywhere. "Praise God," she said in her heart and mind, "this must be answered prayers." She was scared. She did not hear the sirens or any knocking anymore. So, she bravely went towards the door again. It was clear; no one was in the hallway. She slowly tiptoed out the door, scared but bold. She ran as fast as she could, not knowing where she was going, trying to escape.

Trying to find the nearest main road because it was a dirt road where she was being held, and it was now getting dark. She hurried as fast as she could while she was able to see, trying to find any main roads, carefully dodging.

Finally, she found a main road, and as she looked ahead in the distance, she decided not to go directly on it because she was still very close to where she was abducted and held. She was scared. As she continued to walk on the side of the road at a fast pace, hiding and observing her surroundings, she did not want anyone from the area possibly linked with the kidnappers to see or recognize her. She was very afraid that there may be possible connections to hold her captive again. She continued walking until it was dark. She was looking for any shops that might be open that she could go in and ask for help. Gabriel walked for miles in the pitch-black darkness. It was so dark she could not see her hand in front of her face. She was very afraid. She eventually found an abandoned building just off the main road. She prayed that she would be safe staying there for the night because the distance was too long, and it was dark, and she was already tired. She hid in the building for the night. There was a bed and an old broken recliner chair she was able to sit on, although it was dark. There, in the old, abandoned house, she was still able to see and look around because there was a light pole in the backyard. For some reason, the light was on and was bright enough to see inside the house. She looked around, and it was clear, clear enough. Though she was afraid, she was able to rest in the abandoned building. She felt peace come over her because she was free, not being held hostage against her will. Then she prayed to the Lord for protection before she fell asleep. "Dear Lord, thank you for answering my prayers. I did not know it would come this way, but I am thankful. You opened the doors for my freedom. As I lay my head down to sleep, Holy Spirit, cover and shield me with your protection and love while I sleep. Have my guardian angels present to protect me while I sleep. Amen. Oh, yes, my Father, also guide my footsteps as I awaken in the morning and as I go. Go ahead of me and lead me where I need to get help and wherever I go to find my way home. In Jesus' name. Amen."

As soon as Gabriel sat down on the old recliner, she fell asleep because she was so very tired after the long walk. Her feet were aching, and her back too. As Gabriel slept, it got cold, and she shivered and was afraid. Then she felt warmth come over her. She was able to go back to sleep. Then, a short time after, she had a dream. She saw a light that stood by her side, and she was very afraid once again. Then there was a soft voice that spoke with her and said, "Gabriel, don't be afraid. I am your guardian angel. I am always by your side to protect you. Even when you can't see me, I can see you. Don't be afraid; I am here to make sure you are safe, and nothing can or will harm you. You are the apple of His eye, specially selected and chosen because of your heart and love for others. And the Lord, He is with you. Be at peace, my child. Rest well. All is well. You will find your way home." So, Gabriel was awakened for a moment, and she realized it was a dream and fell back to sleep until morning. The sun rose and peeked through the window, and she got up and briefly remembered someone speaking with her. She now knew it was a dream. She carefully looked around and then slowly peeked out the window. Everything was clear. Then she walked towards the door. That was clear too. Then she snuck out, walking towards the bank of the sidewalk.

She walked, refusing anyone who tried to stop and offer her a ride because she was very afraid after the ordeal she had gone through for a few weeks. So, she walked until she saw a restaurant and went in to try to ask for help. But due to how tattered and dirty she looked they thought she was homeless, trying to beg for food. They just chased her away and did not listen to anything she had to say.

Gabriel cried as she walked out and wiped the tears away from her eyes. She continued walking once again, looking around just to make sure no one was watching or following her. At this time, she was very hungry, tired, and weak because she had nothing to eat since the previous day. But she continued walking. It was just about a mile when, just up ahead of her, was what appeared to be a supermarket. She hurried in as she looked towards the counter for someone to help her. She noticed a young woman admiring her as if she knew her. She then walked over and spoke, "Excuse me, Madam! May I help you?" with a smile on her face. The young woman recognized her from a picture her cool volunteers and family had put in the store just in case she would show up. By the time the young woman spoke again, Gabrielle passed out from exhaustion, stopping being tired, weak, and hungry.

They attempted to wake her up and attended to her while the young woman notified the police department about her arrival. The police came quickly. While they were attending to her, she was finally awakened and was able to talk and eat and tell them who she was. The police officer and Gabriel thanked the store owners, and they took her to the hospital to be evaluated and examined. They were asking her many questions about what happened to her during the kidnapping ordeal. She told the officers she could not recognize the faces because they were wearing masks, but she did recognize the baby from the clinic that she volunteered in.

While the doctors, nurses, and counselors attended to her, they called her family and fellow volunteers who were staying in the hotel a few miles away. They were so happy to hear the good news. They spoke with her briefly and cried, praising God for her safe return. Her sister and mother shouted, "We will be there shortly," and hung up. The doctors checked her out. She was okay and was cleared to go. While the police officers continued to ask questions for further investigation, she was very tired. She was very tired but was happy while she rested on her bed. She told the police officers she would be staying for further questioning for further investigation. The hospital staff was very courteous and kind to her and treated her with dignity and respect.

They also had a picture in the hospital lobby. Finally, the police officers left, and she was able to talk more with the nurse who gave her food to eat, a gown, and towels, shampoo, and soap to take a shower. She quickly did. She took a long shower and washed her hair to look presentable for her family and friends, and co-volunteers.

It took a while before they arrived at the hospital. But Gabriel used the time to rest and thank the Lord for keeping her safe and guiding her in the right direction, as he promised. She finally remembered the dream she had had the night before with the Angel. She was happy and thanked the Lord even more.

It was about an hour later. Her family arrived at the hospital, including her co-volunteers. They hugged and kissed her and cried. The volunteers did not stay too long because they knew she needed time to spend with her family. Gabriel thanked them for all the time they spent looking for her and posting pictures all over the place. They excused themselves shortly, respectfully giving her family their time to spend with her since they recently flew down from such a far distance. So, they kissed her goodbye and decided to talk with her another time. Her family, her mom, her sister, her aunt, hugged, kissed, and cried. All of them held hands and prayed, thanking God for bringing her home safely while they talked. She rested. She talked briefly about what happened because she was tired and still shaken by what had happened to her.

"Sometimes when things are falling apart, they may actually be falling into place."

- Unknown

7 THE PLEA

As she tried to rest that evening, she reminisced about the entire ordeal of the kidnapping. She wondered if she had done anything wrong, why they targeted her to be taken. She was also very happy they did not wound or kill her. She cried tears of joy and tears of remorse. Her family spent the night by her side in the hospital. Gabrielle was exhausted but could not sleep. They comforted her and encouraged her to try to sleep, but the nurse came in and gave her some medications for rest.

The next morning, she remembered the baby boy. She was now concerned that they were going to find out who was behind this kidnapping. She called the police officers and requested that once they find out who the child's father was, not to lock him up but to have the judge evaluate him for counseling. She stated it was because of the trauma he suffered from the loss of his wife during the birth of the child. So, she requested this for him. She forgave him for the kidnapping and the weeks she lost. This was what Gabrielle told the police.

"Oh my," they exclaimed, "You are a different kind of woman! You forgave him for what? He did to you?" "Yes," Gabrielle replied, "I believed that man was truly traumatized from the loss of his wife. So, the hurt, his pain, and anguish, him being worried about how this child was going to be taken care of and who is going to support his growth to become a man without a mother. I believe it caused him to do it. This thing he did. I feel his pain and feel bad for him and the child."

The officer was lost for words. He told her he could only write what she says and requesting, but it was up to the judge if he was found. "Thank you, Officer," Gabriel replied and hung up the phone. Then, she said a prayer. "Lord, I pray for him and the child. I pray for the right judge who will have compassion and mercy on him. Thank you for hearing my heart's cry."

She rested for about another half an hour, but her mind was not at rest due to the situation. And shortly after, her family woke up. Her co-volunteer workers needed to see her to say goodbye because they were ready to leave the country and return home. She got up quickly and ran to the door when she heard a knock at the door. She was very happy to see them. Hugs, kisses, and tears of joy. They wanted to say goodbye because they were ready to leave the country and return home.

They talked about how much they prayed for her while she was gone and how happy they were that she came back alive and well. They exchanged phone numbers and email addresses so they could stay in contact with each other. So, the entire family was now awake, and since this was the last day before they left to go home, they decided they were all going to the cafeteria for breakfast and have a proper farewell. They brought her balloons, cards, and small gifts, welcoming her back safely. They had many boxes of tissues because of the tears of joy they felt.

They had breakfast, talked for about two hours, and said their final farewells. Gabrielle, still a bit tired from the ordeal, needed more rest. As the volunteer group walked away and waved goodbye, a tall, dark, and handsome man walked into the room with more flowers, cards, and balloons. It was a surprise. It was Daniel, her close friend. He had waited for the right moment to visit because he wanted to spend quality time with her.

With tears in his eyes, he ran to her. "Gabrielle!" he exclaimed, kissing and embracing her tightly. "Are you well? How are you doing? Are you hurt in any way? Everyone was worried about you."

Gabrielle broke down, started to cry, and held him close. "Thank you for coming. I was not expecting you."

"I thought I lost you. Thank God," Daniel replied.

"Daniel, I am so happy to see you. Thanks for coming," Gabrielle said.

The family praised Daniel, and her sister explained that it was Daniel who had paid for their flight to come and search for her. "Thank you," Gabrielle replied, and the family thanked him once again. They then excused themselves to give Daniel and Gabrielle some privacy.

Tears of joy and happiness flowed as Gabrielle and Daniel held each other's hands tightly. She explained what had happened during the ordeal. Daniel replied, "Now you are safe. The Lord brought you back to us." They talked for a while, cried tears of joy, hugged, and kissed each other.

Daniel stayed and had breakfast, even though Gabrielle had already eaten. Shortly after that, they all met back in her hospital room because Gabrielle was ready to be discharged. She was ready to go.

Gabriel was finally cleared and was released on their own recognizance. So, they drove together in one vehicle to the hotel. While they walked to their vehicle, Daniel held Gabrielle's hand tightly and smiled. She was happy to see him and was finally free. They arrived at the hotel, sat, and talked for a while with her mom, sister, and aunt. They stood beside her and held her, comforted, and supported her with encouraging words. They laughed together. This was the first time she laughed in a while since the ordeal. Daniel, who was standing across the hall, walked with him, held his hand, kissed, and hugged him. She told him how much she cared for and appreciated him, supporting, loving her, and standing by her side with her family. It was now getting late because they hung out all afternoon till the evening. And now it was late night, so she said good night because she was now exhausted. She embraced each of her family members. She wanted them to know how much she appreciated them, loving her and being there for her. She said good night, went to bed, and fell asleep. Early the next morning, they went to a local restaurant outside of the hotel and had breakfast together. But Gabrielle had a worried or concerned look on her face.

Gabriel's mom spoke with her about it. Her mom replied and said, "Gabrielle, I know that look on your face. What's bothering you? Honey! What's on your mind?" And pulled and held her close. Putting her head on her shoulders and gently rubbing her shoulders. She said reluctantly, "I slept well last night, seeing that I was now free. For the past few weeks, but I have this burden on my mind in reference to this child's father who kidnapped me." "Yesterday at the hospital joined my interview, I told the officer I did not want to press charges. I want the father of the baby boy not to be locked up. I would prefer it if they gave him some kind of help and counseling because it would be a tragedy. And their loss, seeing the child already lost. It's mother. And to lose his father also. In jail. It would be a major tragedy. Now this child would lose both parents. It does not make any sense to me." "Well said," her mom replied. "That is the heart of gold. That's my daughter! Always thinking of others instead of herself. Do what You feel Is best. That is in your heart, Daughter," her mom said. Then, Gabriel said, "Because when they do find him and have the arrangement. I will not be here. And I will not be returning for a court trial. So, I was thinking of writing a letter to the judge requesting counseling instead of prison. So. He can. Be a father. To the child. I think this would be best. And the officer also mentioned that he could only take the written statement. What? I was saying. At the interview. And requested. It. But him. Cannot guarantee what the judge's decision will be." Then her sister replied and said, "Gabrielle. I. Think. That's a great idea. To have it in writing. And give it to the police. Superintendent, and. Or Sergeant. to have it on file, so when the arrangement comes. And see what the judge's decision would be." Then Gabrielle says thanks to her mom and sister because it was a heavy load on her mind and heart. So, let me get busy and start to write. The letter. Of request.

Shortly after, someone knocked at the door. It was Daniel. "Good morning. May I come in?" he asked. "Oh, yes," they replied, asking if it was too early. "No, not at all," he responded. "We have been up and talking," the mother added. "Oh, that's great," he replied. "Has everyone had breakfast yet?" "Yes, we had a small amount of food just to hold us over," Gabriel replied as she walked over to greet him.

"Good morning! What are you doing now?" he asked. "Do you remember the conversation we had yesterday at the hospital about the father of the baby?" she inquired.

"Certainly, yes, I do," he replied. "I spoke with the officer on his behalf to get counseling instead of incarceration. I decided to request the same in writing to the judge so that when the time arrives, it won't be a problem since I won't be here," she explained. "That is a splendid idea, a wonderful idea, Gabrielle," Daniel exclaimed. "I agree. I believe it will be much easier, less hassle, and since it is in writing, it will be on file. I think I will also have it notarized. As I stated, I will not be returning for any trials," she said.

"That's a great idea," he replied. "So let me finish writing this letter. When we head out on the road, I will find a place to have it notarized and drop it at the police station to put in his file."

"That makes sense," her sister replied, "because they will be leaving the island soon."

Gabrielle hurried and completed writing the letter. They all headed out for breakfast. As they drove down the street, the police department was about three minutes away, so they stopped there. Gabrielle and Daniel went in while her sister, mom, and aunt waited in the car. Gabrielle requested to speak with the superintendent in charge and had the letter notarized and placed in his record.

Then she thanked the Superintendent. And said goodbye.! And they left. It was a quick visit because. Everything was already. Noted and. On record. Since the previous day. So, they left. Out of the. Police Department and headed. Towards the nearest restaurant. That they could all. Agree on. To have. Being. Peaceful and relaxing. Breakfast. So, on the way. They all talked about how everyone slept last night! They were more concerned about Gabrielle. So. Daniel asked. If she slept well? She replied, I'm a bit restless due to the situation. But well, enough, because. She was now free.

"OK, that's good to hear," Daniel said as he pulled her close and kissed her on her hand and forehead. They finally arrived at the restaurant they had all agreed on. They sat down and ordered their breakfast. The service was excellent, and the food was ready in no time. They ate, talked, and laughed. "We really missed you," her sister said.

"And we were very worried about you." "We all were," her mother and aunt replied.

"The conversation was cut short, but thank the Lord, He kept you safe. Now we are all here, eating, laughing, and talking. It could have been the other way around, so I truly thank God," her mom added.

They all agreed. Her mom saw the pain in Gabrielle's eyes as she said that, and her expression each time she was reminded of all that had taken place. Then she asked, "Baby, are you sure you are, okay?" Gabrielle replied, "Yes," but her mother knew better. Daniel, very observant as well, said to her, "If there is anything I can do, please let me know. If you just want to talk or need space, I am here to listen." He reassured her. She said, "Thanks to all of you. I know you are all just concerned, care, and love me for all I have been through." "Yes, sweetheart," her mom said. "I agree too, Bree," her sister uttered, using the nickname she gave her when they were kids.

"You are going to be just fine," Daniel replied, being optimistic. Her sister changed the subject by telling her about one of her favorites shows that has been going on. So, she drowns her thoughts in that conversation. She laughed and was happy to hear what was going on. They had a great breakfast. Especially Gabriel. She enjoyed it because it had been a while since she had her favorite meal.

Gabriel had lost quite a bit of weight because she did not eat very well while she was being held. The kinds of food they gave her were not the best and not what she was used to eating. So, coming back to a normal meal was just up her alley. They completed breakfast, left the restaurant, and complained of being stuffed. Shortly after, they went back to the hotel to relax and pack for the next day of departure.

"Oh, I am so sorry," Gabriel Replied. "I almost forgot. To say thank you all for coming and assisting in the search. For me. Passing out Flyers. With my pictures so I was able to be found." "It wasn't a problem at all. Sweetheart," her mom replied. Then her sister. And aunt. Said we. Would do it again. If we had! "Yes!" Danielle agreed. "It was my pleasure." So, they stopped by the hotel. To drop off her mom's sister and aunt. And stop by to see. The fellow new volunteers, that will be taken over. She Greeted them and wished them all the best.

"Love isn't something you find;
Love is something that finds you."

- Loretta Young

8 A QUIET PLACE TO TALK

Once they left the hotel, Daniel requested a serene and peaceful place to relax and talk. He suggested a botanical park located a few miles from the hotel. Because at the current time, it had been a few weeks and things had cleared up from the hurricane, especially in the cities and towns. Gabriel said yes. She loved flowers, and it had been a while since she had been out and about, missing the parks that she loved so much. "This is a great idea! Thanks for being so thoughtful," she said to Daniel.

"You are welcome," he replied. "I brought you here because I want you to be comfortable and totally relax." "Thanks," Gabriel replied. Then she asked, "So, would you like to talk about anything? Anything that is on your mind that has been bothering you from your ordeal? If you want to talk about it, I am all ears. Or if you feel more comfortable speaking with a professional, I could recommend a few friends I know. Because I understand you have been through a traumatic event, and it's good to speak with someone. But only when you are ready." "Thanks for caring about me," she replied. "I will think about it and let you know."

"Yes, I was so worried and bothered when I heard what had happened to you. We were all worried about you, but I was praying for you. I asked God to put an edge of protection around you so no harm would come to you, and the Guardian Angels would be with you as well," Daniel said. "I was scared and afraid," Daniel replied. "I cried when I heard the bad news." "Oh wow," said Gabrielle. "I did not think you felt that deeply about me." "Yes, I do," Daniel replied. "It was only after you left and this happened to you that I knew and truly felt what I was feeling, and I could not just sit and do nothing. So, I spoke with your mom and sister, and I told them what my plans were and what their plans were, and they wanted to come along. So, I planned and took care of everything, and we have been here now for two weeks, looking for you and handing out flyers." "Thank you," Gabrielle replied softly. "That was wonderful. Thank you for caring," she sobbed, wiping away the tears. "Please don't cry, Gabrielle," Daniel replied. "Please don't cry." They stopped walking around and stood still, and he held her, wiping away her tears.

They walked to a bench close by and sat as he comforted her and reassured her. Gabriel then placed her head on his shoulder, and he held her close, holding her hand. "I will be OK," she said. "It will be

OK," he reassured her. They sat for about two hours and talked; the hours flew by fast, and it was now close to 6:00 PM. "Gabrielle?" "Yes, Daniel?" she replied. "Are you hungry? Or would you like something to drink?" "No, I am not hungry, but a bit thirsty, and I would love to have a drink."

"Are you not going to eat for the rest of the day?" he asked. "I am not very hungry yet," she replied. "I am a bit hungry. So, what you can do is you can pick a place and choose the food you would like to eat later, and we will pick it up and take it along for later. And when you are ready to eat, it's here." "Yes, Gabrielle," said. "That is a good idea." So shortly afterward, they left the botanical park and went to the restaurant of their choice and had it take-out. While Danielle set an 8 because he was hungry, she just had a cup of peach iced tea. "Thanks, I was thirsty, and thanks for consoling me and for your advice on counseling," she replied.

"After I finish eating, I will drop you off at the hotel. I have quite a bit of packing to do," Daniel said. "I do as well," Gabriel replied. "Then she said, "I so enjoyed the day with her mom and sister, of course, you as well. You top it off. But I do feel much better after talking with you. I so much appreciate you and the advice you gave me. Once again, I am truly grateful."

They returned to the hotel, and Gabriel said, "I will call you later before I go to bed." "Okay," he replied. So, they went back to the hotel and started to pack. Her mom and sister were already packed, so they helped her for a while. They talked, and she talked about the wonderful day she had mentioned the beautiful botanical park. She told them she had a wonderful time and enjoyed her day. Her mom and sister replied, "I am happy you were able to get out."

They talked until they finished packing. "That was quick," Gabriel said. "Certainly was," replied her sister. "Now that I am finished packing, I will go and help Daniel with his. I will see you later." "Okay," they replied. So as Daniel packed, there was a knock at the door. "Hmm, I wonder who that could be?" "Who is it?" he asked. "It's Gabrielle." "Gabrielle? Is everything okay?" he asked as he opened the door. "Yes, everything is okay. Did you forget something?" "Yes, I forgot to take my dinner." "Oh yes," he replied. "Sorry, sorry, I hope I didn't disturb you." "I did not come for the food specifically," Gabrielle replied. "I forgot all about that." "I stopped by to help you pack." "Pack?" he replied. "Don't you have your own packing to do?" "Yes, it's already done. My sister and my mom helped me, and I'm all done." "Well, thank you for being so nice and considerate. That is so thoughtful of you," he said to Gabrielle. "Not a problem at all," she replied. "Are you sure you don't mind?" she asked. "No, not at all," Daniel answered. "Besides, I enjoy your company," he said with a smile on his face. "I enjoy yours as well. Thank you for stopping by and offering to help," she replied. "You're welcome," he said. "So, what's your favorite color?" she asked him. "White and blue are my favorite colors." "Okay, that's nice," she said. "I am sure you look good in them as well," she complimented him.

"We are almost done folding and putting my clothes away," then he said. "I am so happy you are here with me today. Just think a few weeks ago I almost lost you! I wouldn't know what I would do if I had lost you." Then those words sparked and triggered some emotions within her, and she started to cry again. "What have I done! What did I say? I am so sorry to make you cry." "It's okay," she replied, as Daniel drew closer to console, comfort, and dry her tears with a box of tissue that was sitting on the nightstand and gave her a few to hold. He embraced her with a kiss on her forehead and held her close, holding her hand tightly. "I am sorry," he replied. "I didn't mean to make you cry. But it's hard not thinking about what happened to you!" Gabriel spoke and said, "It's true."

Then she turned and passionately kissed him on his lips while she gently caressed his face and kissed his neck and head. Gabriel expressed her feelings as well, that she missed him and thought of him a few times but was not sure if he had moved on since then. "Are you crazy?" he replied. "That evening at the beach, I could not stop thinking about you. I couldn't take you out of my mind and heart. You have been there since, but you left, and I figured I would keep it hidden until you return home. Now here we are." They talked and kissed, embracing each other passionately.

"Love is a tender touch, that ignites the sparks of one's heart."

- Angela Griffiths

9 THE UNPLANNED SEXUAL ENCOUNTER

Gabriel was sweating from the afternoon at the Botanical Park. She needed a change of clothes but also needed to soak and relax in the tub. Daniel ran her bath water with fragranced soap. He excused himself as she went in and took her clothes off, then sat in the bathtub, which was large enough for two, relaxed her head on the headrest, and closed her eyes.

Daniel was excited and couldn't stay away much longer. He came in and poured water on her long, black, silky hair, washing it as she lay relaxed in the tub. Then he washed her back and bathed her, washing her feet. She was completely relaxed. Then he kissed her slowly and gently on her forehead, gradually moving to her neck, then her lips. She held him tightly, kissing him back passionately, holding his head and neck towards her lips. She held him tightly with passion in her eyes. She stood up and released the water out of the tub to take a shower and wash the soap away from her body.

Then Daniel stepped into the shower and caressed her, massaging her shoulders while he embraced and pulled her close, continuing to kiss her neck and back. He massaged her head and neck while kissing her passionately, then caressed her breast and kissed them slowly and gently. She forgot all about crying; instead, he gave her a passionate caress.

Again, he stood behind her and pulled her long black hair to the side, kissing her ears, back, and the back of her neck. She gently moved her neck from side to side and joined the moment, then took his soft hand and caressed her face and outlined her lips with his long, slender fingers, kissing them softly. Then he held her close and tightly from behind and gently penetrated her, her gentle groans, and his passionate moves. Then, slightly, she flexed forward, reaching for the faucet to run warm water once again in the tub. Warm water emerging in it heightened the foreplay. Then she gently pulled him into the large jacuzzi tub, submerging him in the tub with her. Then she straddled him and sat.

They were in heaven on earth! No more tears of pain but tears of joy. "I want all of you," Gabriel whispered. "You have me," Daniel replied. "All of you!" "I want heart, body, and mind. I want to know what makes you happy," then he smiled. Then she quieted herself to focus on loving him as he gently caressed her breast, her lips, and buttocks. She held onto his broad shoulders and chest, caressing and rubbing them, staring into each other's eyes as they were looking through glass to each other's souls.

They finally got out of the jacuzzi, soaking wet. He looked at her and admired her beautiful body silhouette and dried her with a towel hung up in the bathroom. Then he admired her beautiful body and soft skin, giving her compliments on how beautiful she was. "Yes, thank you, and you as well. You're just as handsome," she said, smiling. "As handsome as ever!" He smiled and replied the same. They walked out of the bathroom with the towel wrapped around themselves. Gabriel sat on the bed, overlooking the beautiful landscape of the hotel because they were at the highest level. As she stared out the window, he applied warm, scented body butter on her entire body, gently massaging her from head to toe, from front to back, enticing more lovemaking.

Gabriel stood up and gently massaged and rubbed Daniel's chest and shoulder, applying lotion to his body as well, from head to toe passionately. After that, the kissing, caressing, massaging, rubbing, holding, and embracing started all over again. Kissing his ears turned him on as she headed towards his chest and stomach, causing him to clench his toes. The process continued as she proceeded to kiss him, leading into ecstasy. He imagined what was next.

He was unable to hold himself, and because Daniel was not the selfish kind of man to please himself first or leave his woman wanting, he wanted to please her first, then himself. He pulled her, picked her up, gently placing her on the bed, and caressing her gently, kissing her back and the back of her neck, then her ears with a gentle passion. She screamed as he slowly moved to her back, kissing it softly and in slow motion, then the back of her thighs, rolling her over slowly and from her toes to her inner thighs, teasing her by putting his tongue in her belly button. Then kissing her breasts and massaging them with his fingers and kissing her at the same time, leading her to climax. She took his thumb and finger in her mouth, sucking on them like candy. They both climaxed by teasing each other. He pulled her close to the edge of the bed as he stared into her beautiful eyes and admired her beautiful body. After they were done, Daniel laid next to Gabriel and held her close in his arms as she listened to his heartbeat, and he did the same.

It was already very late. She took a quick shower and got dressed, kissed Daniel, and he kissed her. They embraced each other as he whispered in her ear, "Thank you for a wonderful evening." She replied with the same sentiment, smiles adorning their faces. Then Gabriel spoke, expressing her enjoyment of the evening. "I really enjoyed the evening," she said. Gabrielle followed, adding, "I really enjoyed spending time with you. It has been a while since I've had human touch, especially after all the ordeal I recently went through. I am happy and content." Danielle chimed in, "We enjoyed our time together. You are beautiful inside and out. You made me happy. You make me happy," Gabriel replied gratefully.

Daniel then continued, addressing Gabrielle, "Gabrielle, what I'm going to say, please don't get me wrong. I enjoy your love, your touch, your tenderness. I enjoy everything about you. But I also want to apologize to you because I am feeling a bit guilty about making love to you. Because I know it was not the right way. I am so sorry. I got carried away. God forgive me." He expressed his concerns about taking advantage of her or disrespecting her during times she was most vulnerable. Gabriel reassured him, "I will pray and ask for forgiveness too. I did not feel as though you took advantage of me. It was my choice, free will, and I decided to engage with you. If I did not want to, I wouldn't have, and I would have pushed you away and said no. So please, Danielle, do not feel guilty. And forgive me as well." Daniel acknowledged her words, stating, "There's nothing to forgive. You did not hurt me in any way. But I do understand where you are coming from and why you are apologizing. I know you are a godly man, a man that respects me and God and goes by His laws. But we all make mistakes sometimes. We are flesh and humans. And sometimes we are overtaken by desires, and the flesh gets weak at times."

"Thank you for understanding," Daniel concluded. They communed for a little while longer before realizing it was time to go. Saying goodnight to each other, they hugged, kissed, and held each other for a moment. Daniel then opened the door for her and walked with her across the hall to her hotel room. Her family was waiting, trying to stay awake for her, but they both fell asleep, gently snoring. Gabriel kissed and hugged them goodnight, trying not to wake them up. Then she went into her room to bed. She was unable to sleep immediately, lying there and reminiscing on the encounter that had just taken place. Eventually, she fell asleep until the next morning.

"Have enough courage to trust love,
one more time and always one more time."

- Maya Angelou

10 GOING HOME

Early the next morning, they were all awakened by the alarm. "Good morning," they greeted each other with kisses and hugs, then hurried into the bathroom to wash up quickly and get dressed. They planned to meet downstairs together for breakfast before heading to the airport. "Today is the big day," her mother exclaimed. "We are finally going home!" "Absolutely," Gabriel said, excited and happy.

By the time they were ready and downstairs, Danielle was already waiting for them. "Good morning," he said. They all greeted him warmly, with Gabriel greeting him with hugs, kisses, and holding his hand as they walked to the coffee machine. While he made coffee, she prepared toast and a plate for him.

As they sat down to eat and talk, time was moving fast. When her mom mentioned the time, they realized they needed to hurry and leave soon. After quickly disposing of the unwanted food and garbage, they went upstairs to pick up their luggage, which was waiting at the door. Daniel found a luggage carrier and brought everyone's luggage downstairs to the front door, where they checked out. Then, Daniel packed the luggage into the car while everyone got comfortable and ready to go.

They drove to the airport, returned the rental car, and checked in at the airport counter with ample time to spare. As they sat and waited until the time to board the plane, Danielle remarked, "Wow, we finally made it here." They sat down and talked for a short moment, with her mother and sister sitting close by across from them. Daniel then leaned closer to Gabriel and whispered something in her ear, making her smile. After excusing himself briefly to speak with her mom and sister, he returned to his seat next to Gabriel. She was curious about what they had whispered about, noticing their smiles, but Daniel didn't say a word.

Then, Daniel got up again, went down on one knee, pulled out a small red box from his pocket, and opened it, presenting it to Gabriel. "Gabriel, would you marry me and be my wife?" Gabriel was very surprised and lost for words, speechless as she looked up at him, her mom and sister bursting into tears of happiness and rushing over to hug her and Daniel. "Yes! Yes! Yes! I will marry you," she exclaimed tearfully, hugging, and kissing Daniel before he could say another word.

"This has been a long time coming," Daniel said. "I wanted to do this at the hotel and at the hospital, but it was not the right time. But now it is. I wanted your family present, and these strangers here in the airport to witness my love. I love you, Gabrielle! I have nothing to regret. I waited and almost lost you! And I will never let that happen again. So, I am proposing my love to you today after all the ordeal you went through. I am asking once again; would you marry me and be my wife? I love you!" he declared, kissing her as she burst into tears again, hugging him tightly as he hugged her and cried as well.

"I would love to be your husband," she replied, holding his hands as he placed the beautiful Marquis diamond ring with rose gold on her finger. They looked at it, crying and smiling at the same time, admiring the beautiful ring as he kissed her. Cheers erupted from the people in the airport, with her mom, sister, and aunt giving them hugs, kisses, and congratulations.

Shortly after the proposal, their flight number, 1038, was called for boarding to New York. They lined up, approached the counter, showed their tickets and passports, and were congratulated again before boarding the plane. There were cheers and congratulations, hugs and kisses for their engagement. "You deserve it," her mom said, clapping and cheering as they sat down in the plane. They brought champagne for a toast. Gabriel was still in disbelief that she was actually engaged to be married after all the ordeal she had gone through.

She wasn't expecting this as she sat comfortably in her seat next to her now-fiancé Daniel. As the flight attendants gave instructions for liftoff, they buckled their seat belts and were ready for takeoff. "This is the part I hate," Gabrielle said to Daniel. "Don't worry, my darling," Daniel reassured her. "Everything will be alright." "OK," she replied. "I trust and pray it will be," holding his hand tightly.

As the plane lifted off and leveled off in midair, Gabriel was now at ease, playing with the beautiful ring on her finger as she was deep in thought. Daniel noticed and asked, "Are you alright, my love?" "Yes," she replied. "I am fine. Just something that is very important I need to say." "Oh, OK," Daniel said. "Speak on what's on your mind, my love. There is nothing too hard for me to understand or take time out to listen to you," he replied. "Thank you," Gabriel replied. "We are planning to get married, and because of the time away, we had not had a chance to talk in greater detail and intimacy due to the trip away and what occurred. I don't know how to break the bad news."

"Oh no," he replied. "It doesn't matter. We can handle it together. Please go ahead. I am listening!" "I really don't know how to break the news to you, seeing we are trying to be a family," Gabriel continued. Daniel's heart was beating fast as he waited to hear the worst. Then she said, "I am not able to have children." Daniel's heart dropped, but he held Gabriel close, whispering in her ear, "We can, and we'll get through this too. I love you regardless and despite the circumstances."

Gabriel explained about her past, the reason why she couldn't have children. "While I was married, we tried, and nothing happened. I did not have the opportunity to check with a specialist while we were planning to have children. That's when my ex-husband started becoming abusive towards me, so I called it off." "Oh, sweetheart,"

Daniel replied, showing his sympathy and empathy towards her. "I am so sorry to hear what you went through." My God, he said, "You went through a lot. You have been through quite a bit." Yes, Gabriel replied.

Then, Daniel said once again, "I am so sorry to hear. But we will go through this as well! We will go through this together." Then he suggested, "We can always adopt if you desire to do so." "Certainly," she replied, uplifted with joy, excitement, and relief. "That is a splendid idea." She smiled and then kissed Danielle. As they talked a little about wedding plans, she was even more excited because it had been years since her last marriage due to her fear of engaging in another relationship after her past devastating and abusive one.

But it had been years, and she decided to step out on faith despite her past. Plus, Daniel was a different man, an honest, humble, and God-fearing man, a loving person who was kind, generous, and encouraging to her, a leader who could lead her to make the right decisions, peaceful, and always positive and happy no matter what was happening in his life. He was the kind of person she had been waiting for, the one the Lord had promised in a dream and sent her way. She had dreamt of him several times but was not sure how or even when this would happen until one day, out of the clear blue skies, he appeared and found her when she least expected it and at the time when she needed someone to talk to, someone who understood and had similar experiences.

He was the type of person who used wisdom, common sense, and discernment, very wise and smart, sensitive, and made her laugh, and she made him laugh as well. It was several hours before they landed and arrived in the US, tired from the long journey. They continued to talk, served snacks and drinks, and watched movies until they fell asleep for hours. They woke up, played games, and listened to music to pass the time. Daniel wanted to talk to Gabriel about the unplanned sexual encounter, which weighed heavily on his mind and heart, feeling guilty about it happening and wanting to discuss it with her, but it didn't seem like a good time.

He figured they could find a quiet place and time to discuss it once they got home and settled. A few romantic love songs played, stimulating their thoughts as they gently held each other tightly, whispering sweet nothings in each other's ears and laughing. They were about three hours away from home and looking forward to finally getting off the airplane. Her sister and mother were a few seats ahead of them, and once again, the talk of marriage came up. Gabrielle was very happy, never having been this happy in a long time, and Danielle was also very happy, as it had been a long while for him as well since his last marriage relationship, which had also failed. So, they both had experience in a failed relationship.

"Try to be a rainbow in someone else's cloud"

- Maya Angelou

11 THE LOOK

After all the talk, laughter, and affirmation, there was a look in Gabriel's eyes that Daniel could pick up, indicating that there was something more on her mind. He was sensitive in reading her thought sometimes, sensing when something was wrong, but he couldn't quite put his finger on it. He asked, "Gabrielle, is there something else on your mind you want to disclose?"

"Why do you ask?" she replied. Daniel said, "I discerned something more is bothering you! It's all over your face." "I did not realize my emotions showed on my face. I am trying hard not to talk about this, but yes, it still bothers me. What is bothering You?" Daniel asks. "What is it, my love? You know I am here for you, a listening ear, a shoulder to cry on," Danielle replied softly.

Gabriel acknowledged it and said yes. She knows this is the time to put everything on the table, since they are now engaged. "Yes, my love,"

Daniel replied softly as he pulled closer to her and laid their hands on his lap, patiently waiting for her to begin speaking.

As she reminisced and started to talk with Daniel, Gabriel said, "I am angry and still hurt! When will all this go away? This is the reason for my calamity, this is the reason for my suffering, and this is the reason that caused me to be infertile." As Daniel stayed quiet and listened to her, he felt her pain and hurt as the words came forth out of her mouth. But all he did was to stay quiet and listen so she could vent.

He knows a good counselor that he could recommend who listens without interruptions. So, as she continued to talk, he again held her hands and listened! Then, she said, "I was a teenager when this happened to me. My uncle at the time had a so-called friend next door where we lived at the time. Every day I came home from school, he seemed to be a very nice guy. He would pick up his son, and I would walk home. He would offer a ride home, and I would take a ride because I knew him, and he was my uncle's best friend. All that talk, laughter, and affirmation. There was a look in Gabriel's eyes. That Daniel could pick up. That there was something more on her mind! He was sensitive in reading her when something was going on or when something is wrong. But he could not put his finger on it. He asked, "Gabrielle is there something else on your mind you want to disclose?" Why do you ask, she replied. Daniel. Said, "I discerned something more is bothering you. It's all over your face." I did not realize my emotions showed on my face. I am trying hard not to talk about this but yes, it is still bothering me. "What is bothering you, Daniel asks? What is it my love?" You know I am here for you and listening ears, a shoulder to cry on.

Gabriel knows this is the time to put everything on the table since we are now engaged. Yes, my love, Daniel. replied softly as he pulled closer to her and laid their hands on his lap, held her hands while patiently waiting for her to begin speaking.

As she reminisced and started to talk with Daniel, Gabriel says, "I am angry and still hurt! When will all this go away? This is the reason for my calamity! This is the reason for my suffering! This is the reason that has caused me to be unfertile. As Daniel stayed quiet and listened to her, he felt her pain and hurt as the words came forth out of her mouth. He stayed quiet and listened so she could vent. He knows a good counselor that he could recommend listening without interruptions. As she continued to talk, he again held her hands and listened! She said "I was a teenager when this happened to me. My uncle, at the time, had a so-called friend next door where we lived. Every day when I came home from school, he seemed to be a very nice guy, picking up his son. I would walk home, and he would offer me a ride home. I would accept the ride because I knew him, and he was my uncle's best friend.

He frequently visited his house to play cards and other games. However, all I did was say hello and occasionally accept the ride home. My uncle was a womanizer, often attempting to slap me on the bottom as I passed by. I disliked it and tried to avoid walking near him as much as possible. Despite this, I didn't think much of it. Naively, I simply ran away whenever I saw him because I knew he might try to slap me again.

One day I was home, and my dad was having a heart attack. I did not know what to do. So, I ran to the neighbor's house, knocked on the door, calling for help. No one was answering the door, but the door was unlocked. I noticed as I pushed it, it opened. My uncle's friend's car was in his driveway, and his friend's car was also parked in the driveway. So, I was happy to know someone was home. I pushed the door open, calling for help, and fell down as I pushed the door. I opened the wrong door that leads to the basement. I lost my balance and fell down the stairs and fell in and out of consciousness. But I could hear voices laughing and talking. It was dark. I called for help but could not see around me. When I was conscious, I was bleeding because I hit my head while I was falling towards the bottom of the steps. At times, I thought I heard footsteps, but I was not sure. I also was unable to get up and walk because I dislocated my left hip.

I was in severe pain and in and out of consciousness. While I was unconscious, lying on the floor, someone raped me. I was trying to scream and fought them off. But I was in severe pain and was too weak to fight. I passed out again from the pain and the injury to my head. "Oh my God!" Daniel said, while Gabriel cried. He held her tight and comforted her. He apologized to her for the evil that was done to her. "My dear Gabriel! Oh God, you have suffered terribly. Many bad things have befallen you," as he wiped away the tears from her eyes and consoled her.

Then he asked, "Did they find him?" in an angry tone. "And who did it?" She answered yes. "After I was found, went to the hospital, and was able to talk, I told them I was raped. But they did not believe me. They said I had a bad fall, was in and out of consciousness for a while, were in a pool of blood, and very lucky to be alive. They did not believe me. They raped me and left me there."

Oh, my Lord Daniel replied. Once again, he was speechless through this ordeal. He didn't know what to say but to console her and hug her. The only thing he said was, "That was horrible!" A few weeks later, I realized I was pregnant. I did not have a boyfriend, and I was a virgin. Now the police were involved, and a major investigation and testing were done. After the investigation, it was discovered that it was my neighbor's son.

Daniel gasped in disbelief and was hurting Gabriel. In the end, she lost the baby because of the severe injuries and the stress of the whole situation. I am so sorry to hear you have gone through so many ordeals, including this one, he said. She just nodded her head as he held her close, kissed her, and told her everything would be alright. What had become of your father, he asked." She replied, "He had a major stroke from the heart attack. He died a year later. The stress and circumstances pulled him down and eventually caused his death."

"How did your mom and sister take it?" he asked. "It was hard on my mom. My sister was too young to understand," Gabriel replied. "Oh, my love. Once again, I am so sorry. I am here for you anytime you want to talk. I am here to listen," Yes, Gabriel responded. I was doing very well. But with this recent kidnapping, it brought back some old memories." Then Daniel said, "I will do my best to love and cherish you. If you need more counseling, go ahead. Actually, I would love for you to go, if you have no objections." She said OKAY! She remained silent for the rest of the flight home.

"Love is like the wind, you can't see it,
but you can feel it."

- Nicholas Sparks

12 THE ARRIVAL HOME

They finally arrived home, landing in New York City. Her sister and Mom yelled, "Yay! It has been a while," Gabriel said. "Yes, we are finally home," Daniel started praising the Lord. "We arrived home safely," her mother replied. "Yes, and thank God," her sister added. Everyone stood up in their seat and started pulling off their luggage from the overhead racks as the plane pulled closer to the hangar spot.

As the plane completed its stop and the doors were opened, everyone hurried to get off the plane because it had been a long ride. They waited in line to head outside down to the luggage Carousel. Daniel, Gabriel, her mom, and sister hugged each other while waiting at the carousel. They were exhausted, and many of the people who were on the flight hugged them and congratulated them once again, saying goodbye. Finally, the luggage arrived on the rack, and they pulled them off one by one. Then Daniel found a luggage rack and packed all the bags and suitcases on it, pushing it outside to the upper section of the garage where his truck was parked.

He noticed that Gabriel was not speaking as much. So, he left her alone, observing and offering help in any way he could. They arrived at the truck, unloaded the luggage in the trunk of his vehicle. Then he opened the door for the women to be seated and neatly packed the luggage in the trunk of his vehicle. He started to drive Gabriel's mom and sister home, which was about an hour's drive from the airport. He was very concerned about Gabriel because her demeanor had changed, and now she was very quiet.

Her mom and sister were quiet too, and they noticed she was very quiet when they arrived at the airport. They talked while he was driving, trying to make conversation, listening to music so the time could pass. Eventually, they made it home. Gabriel's mom asked if she was okay. She said she was, but her actions suggested something else. Her demeanor had certainly changed. So, her mom pulled Daniel aside and spoke with him and agreed to recommend professional help for counseling. He agreed.

Daniel knew a few professional people he could recommend to her mom, and she trusted his judgment and opinion. Then they spoke with Gabriel, and she agreed to go. Then they said they would support her all the way until things got better. Her mom replied, "And so said Samuel and her sister." She kissed her, hugged her, and consoled her, letting her know that everything would be alright. She told her that God had seen her through all this time and now he's not going to leave her. Then she welcomed her home.

"On Tuesday, I will call and schedule an appointment for you," her mom replied. "Is that okay?" Gabriel said, "Yes, it is, Mom! Thank you all for caring about me." Daniel hugged her and said, "We all care about you! And I love you, sweetheart." He pulled her aside and sat in the living room as soon as he unpacked their luggage from the vehicle. Then Daniel said, "I will support you all the way through this. You will get through this. You will get the help you need. I will be there for you! I am repeating myself because I want you to understand and believe what I am telling you. I am here for you. We will put on hold any wedding plans for now until you are better. I don't want any additional stress and pressure on you. I will come and be at every appointment if you want me to be there." "Certainly," she replied. "We will wait a few weeks and continue wedding plans if you are okay with that?" She replied, "Yes, it is okay. I want to be well and happy for my wedding. You are such a considerate man. Thank you," he replied. "I tried to be. I will come in or wait outside. But whatever you choose, I will be there. With and for you." "Thank you, Daniel. Thank you," she cried and reached over to hug him. "Not a problem," he said. "It's my pleasure," as he consoled her again, wiping away tears from her eyes. Then Daniel wanted reassurance that she was okay with putting off the wedding plans for now until after she completed her counseling. She spoke and said, "Yes, it's okay. Whatever you think is best. Right now, I am fine with it. I also believe so as well," as she looked at her beautiful ring on her finger. "It's so beautiful. You have exquisite taste," she replied. Then Daniel said, "Thank you, but not as beautiful as you!" She smiled. Then he said, "I enjoy seeing you smile." "Thank you, My love," Gabriel replied. Then he hugged and kissed her and said goodnight. "I must be going now. It's getting late, and I am exhausted. And I know you are too, and you need to rest. I have an hour's drive," then she said, "I understand. Please get home safely. I will give you a call as soon as I arrive home." "Sounds great," she replied. She held his hand as she walked him to the door on the porch and to his vehicle. He waved and said good night to her mom and sister at the door. She embraced him tightly once again, kissed him, and said good night. But there was sadness in her eyes as if she did not want him to go. Daniel whispered in her ear, "It won't be long. You will be my wife very soon. And we will be together soon," and gave her a long kiss. "I will also pick you up on Tuesday," as he stepped up into his truck. He said, "We will talk soon," waved goodbye, and drove away.

She walked back into the house. Her mom reminded her about the appointment as she closed the door behind her. "Sounds great," she said. "Have a good night, Gabriel," as she hugged and kissed her and her sister. It was her first night back home in her own room. She was happy and very excited to be home with her family. She stayed in the living room with her mom and sister as she watched the time, awaiting Daniel's call.

The family talked, laughed, hugged each other, and cried for the joy of not losing Gabrielle. "Okay, mom," she said. "Please don't cry anymore. Make this time special. I am now home and there's nothing to worry or cry about! I am just fine. I am happy to be home. Very happy," she said. "I don't want to think about the things I have been through. I just want to move on and focus on the future? On what is ahead of me!" "That's great," her sister replied. "That is a positive notion," her mom also replied. "I am so proud of you," her sister added. "Well said," Mom replied. "I am proud of you as well."

It was not very long after Danielle called, and she said goodnight to her sister and mom and took the call. He said, "I just made it home. I know it's getting late. I did not want you to wait up for too long. I also know that you are tired because it was a long trip home. You need your rest. Please rest well!" "Thanks for being so caring and observant," Gabriel said. "I know you are tired as well. I would like you to get your rest. I do know you are tired too!" "Yes, I am," he replied. "I love you. Sleep well and have a good night." "I love you too," Gabrielle replied. "Rest well. Have a good night." And they both hung up the phone at the same time. She spoke with the family for a short moment after the call because they were still awake watching television. Then I said goodnight and went to bed. Even though she was tired, she was unable to sleep immediately because this was her first night back home in her own bed.

As she lay in bed, she thought of the long journey where she came from and what had happened to her. She thought about the baby and hoped for the best. She forced herself to sleep by turning the television on and listening to some Christian services until she fell asleep. Early the next morning, her sister and mother got up and made breakfast because they had to return to work. They ate together and then left for work.

"Love has nothing to do with what you are expecting to get-Only what you are expecting to give! Which is everything."

- Katherine Hepburn

13 THE LAKE VISIT

Gabriel didn't have any plans for the day, so she waited until she received a call from Daniel and then planned what to do for the rest of the day. She decided to wait a week before returning to work because she needed to get counseling first. In the afternoon, she decided to go to the park and watch the ducks and swans at the lake. She brought a book to read and stayed most of the early afternoon at the lake. At that time, a few people on their lunch break stopped by and fed the ducks, and a young family across the way was at the picnic table with a young baby boy. This triggered her memory of the baby on the island.

She stopped reading and walked away to clear her thoughts. She left her phone on the bench. It was now late in the evening, and her mom and sister were calling to check on her, but there was no answer. Daniel was also trying to contact her, but she did not pick up his calls either. They were worried about her because it was after 6:00 PM. Danielle was concerned and called her mother, but they were also unaware of her whereabouts. Her sister remembered her love for the lake, so they went there but found no one at the park and it was getting dark. However, her mom spotted a book on the table with Gabrielle's name written on it.

Now they started to worry if something bad had happened to her again. Daniel was very concerned and called her sister, who answered and told him they were at the park looking for Gabrielle and found her book she left on a bench. Daniel said he was on his way and was very anxious and distraught about what was happening. He started to pray as he drove to help find her. "Oh, Father," he proclaimed, "watch over my love, watch and protect Gabrielle wherever she is. Let no harm come upon her. She has suffered hard and long, Lord. I pray, send the angels of protection to guard her, guide her footsteps, and let no harm come to her. Send angels to her side, wherever she is at this time. Oh, God, in the name of Jesus, I pray. Amen."

At this time, her mother and sister decided to drive up and down the local streets to see if she was walking but did not find her. Daniel was speeding to get there, and he was close by, exiting from the highway. It was now dark, and her sister and mom were very worried and shouted and started to cry, not knowing what else to do. Daniel was now consoling them both on the phone and was very positive that she would be found.

He advised them to go home and see if she made it there. They took his advice and did so. As Daniel approached the intersection of the highway, he saw many cars in front of him, slowing down, and some even stopping. As he approached, he wondered what was going on and wanted the traffic to move, but it seemed as if it was moving inch by inch per minute. Since everyone was stopping and getting out of their cars as if there was an accident ahead, he got out as well to see what the hold-up was and what the commotion was about.

As he approached, he saw her sitting on the side of the road with her head and lower lip bleeding and a bruised knee. Someone had called for an ambulance, and Daniel was in disbelief at what he saw. Gabrielle was running away from the people as they tried to approach and help her. His heart dropped in pain when he saw her. Then he called her name, "Gabrielle!" She looked up at him but did not speak, with a look of fear in her eyes, but she stayed with him.

Then he asked the crowd of people what happened to her. The first bystander in his car said she tried to cross the road, and they almost hit her. They tried to protect her from crossing the main street and possibly getting killed, but she seemed very fearful and kept running away. Once again, Daniel called her name, and she looked up at him, smiled, and went to him, holding his arms tightly, shaking.

He called the family and said he had found her. He told the bystanders that he and the family had been looking for her. She sat for him, and he wiped away the blood from her forehead, knees, and lips. He asked her what happened, but she did not answer, just smiled. He asked if she was in pain or hurt, but she just stared and smiled. "Oh, my Lord, my sweet Gabrielle," he said, tears streaming from his eyes as he continued to ask her if she was okay. He thanked everyone, placed her in the car seat, and drove her to the hospital emergency room.

On his way to the hospital, he called her sister and mom again and told them he was on his way to the hospital because she had fallen and had bruises to her head, knees, and lips. They arrived at the hospital ER, and he brought her to the desk. The intake nurse saw her wound and said she needed stitches and an X-ray right away. The doctor examined her, and she seemed to be in some sort of shock, so the doctor ordered an MRI and CT scan of her head and drew blood. The results only revealed superficial cuts and bruises, but she was in some sort of post-traumatic stress. The doctor recommended further evaluation and counseling, so she was kept in the hospital for observation that night.

A few hours later, the blood work results came back negative. Both the CAT scan and MRI results were negative too! "Praise the Lord," they exclaimed. "It's good. Everything's superficial. Hallelujah," Danielle said. Mom echoed the sentiment and shouted. Then the doctor sent her upstairs for the night in a private room. They spent the night by her side at the hospital. She fell asleep quickly because she had pain medication, and she was knocked out. Danielle was very concerned because he loved her so much and wanted to marry her. He desperately wanted her to be his wife. He kissed her on the forehead and hands as she slept.

While her sister and mom slept, he prayed. "Lord, what is happening? I am not questioning You, Lord, but let Your perfect will be done in Gabriel's life and mine! Heal her speedily. Let her recovery be completed. Not partial, but completely. Let her life after this be a testimony for others to hear and see and be blessed! Help me to be strong both for her and the family. I know You know all things, even from the beginning to the end. I thank You, Lord, for hearing and answering my prayers. Amen." Then he fell asleep in his chair.

A few hours later, he was awakened by the collaboration of doctors examining Gabriel. She was the same, with no verbal responses except a smile on her face. After the doctors completed the initial examination, they left. He was able to spend a few moments with her because he had to leave and go home to take a shower, change clothes, and eat. Her mother said the same as they rotated the time and schedule to go home so she would not be alone at the hospital. When one returned, the other would go home and rest. This was done until the end of the 24 hours because they did not want her to be left alone. The 24 hours turned into 72 hours because she wasn't responding.

So, on the second day, they brought in a psychologist who came in and talked with the family and explained exactly what was going on and what needed to be done. Then he talked and counseled her daily. On the third day, they discharged her with the recommendation and prescription to go home with a psychologist he recommended for therapy, three times per week, about an hour session each day at an outpatient clinic, and strongly recommended family support.

Her sister, mom, and Daniel would go with her each week, rotating on a weekly basis. Each one of them would share the responsibility of her care until she recovered. Shortly after the third week, Gabrielle started to respond to therapy verbally. She made a full recovery. This was done so she would not be even more traumatized and less stressed and within more familiar surroundings with loved ones, her family, and friends, instead of putting her in an inpatient facility.

But she continued to follow up for counseling on a regular basis, twice a week. She was able to drive herself and take care of herself with no additional help. She did not remember the incident or what happened at the park when Daniel found her. He explained how she was found. They were all excited and happy, moving forward with their lives and wedding plans. A year later, they got married, and a year following the marriage, they adopted a beautiful baby girl. Their lives were full of joy and happiness. Their life was never the same. 18 months later, Gabriel unexpectedly got pregnant. The Lord blessed them with a son of their own. It was a surprise to both because she was not expected to get pregnant because of the trauma she suffered in her past, the rape. Daniel was in shock as well, but they were very happy. So, they called him Samuel.

Now it was a beautiful summer evening, and the sun was setting over the horizon. It was a yellowish-orange glaze. Gabrielle thanked God as she reminisced on her past, on all that she had been through. Now, she was smiling, joyful, and at peace in her heart, holding his hand as they strolled on the white sandy beach, aqua-blue waters. This is the rest that she had always dreamed of having after the storm, picking up from the broken pieces. She pulled away, walking towards the edge as the waves arrived, touching her toes as she looked out in the distance. Then Daniel came up behind her, picking her up by her waistline, and twirled her around. She laughed and laughed. Then he thought to himself and said, "What have I done to deserve such an angel in my life? Gabrielle, my wife!" Then he embraced her tightly and kissed her passionately, whispering sweet nothings in her ear.

The End

Made in the USA
Columbia, SC
01 November 2024

45141730R00050